DERAILED GEARS

E. ROBERT BROOKS

Also by E. Robert Brooks
Pirouette
Wine Thief
The Concours Caper

Publishing Coordinator – Sharon Kizziah-Holmes
Cover Design – Jaycee DeLorenzo

Paperback-Press
an imprint of A & S Publishing
A & S Holmes, Inc.

ISBN -13: 978-1-951772-63-5

DEDICATION

Mark Mattei- My thanks for his infinite patience in allowing a ratpack of teenagers in the 1970s (of which I was one), to regularly hang out at his bicycle shop, where he taught us brazing and frame building techniques, and honed our abilities to use specialized tools.

Keith Hellon- A self-taught engineer, who thought outside of the box, was unfettered by traditional design limitations, and succeeded in gaining an acclaimed worldwide reputation as a game-changing inventor of automotive components. Keith taught me invaluable mechanical skills, and educated me about the history and evolution of the racing bicycle in Europe.

PROLOGUE

(In cycling, a prologue is a short preliminary time trial held
before a race to establish a leader)

L ate one night, Ernesto Sante was laboring in
his small makeshift workshop to finish
building a custom lightweight steel racing
bicycle frame for famed local racer—Gino Fausto,
who was the favorite to win the upcoming
prestigious *Giro d'Italia* competition.

Sante, who had been nicknamed The Tailor by
the European racing community, was a legendary
builder.

He possessed extraordinary skill at creating short
wheelbase racing frames with stiff, catlike handling,
that, due to the meticulous bespoke measurements
for the rider's physique were surprisingly
comfortable to ride over long distances.

An important attribute for grueling races such as
the *Giro*.

He was a true craftsman, and his frames not only consistently performed well, but were also beautiful to behold.

Unlike the famed French *constructeurs*, who, in the 1950s were for the most part focused on building filet-brazed lugless touring bicycles, with elaborate braze-ons to attach proprietary components- for racing bikes, Italian frames had become the preferred choice amongst many top competitors, and Sante was recognized as one of the elite artisans.

Sante favored bright colors for his frames, devoid of pinstriping and contrasting panels, to highlight his signature Florentine *fleur-de-lis* cutouts, which he engraved by hand in the minimalist hand-shaped and painstakingly filed and finished lugs, with elegant shorelines.

His detailing was much subtler than the complex embellishments favored by many British frame makers at that time, which resembled the elaborate curvilinear designs of fine sterling silver culinary utensils and intricately engraved bespoke shotgun sideplates.

Sante's brazing technique included the use of both bronze rod for the thicker metal of bottom brackets and dropouts, and nickel silver for the much thinner-walled lug joinery.

Most Italian builders used domestically made Columbus tubing exclusively for their projects, but Sante always combined a proprietary mix of both Columbus and British Reynolds tubing for each build, specifically chosen for each rider's physique and the intended use for the frame.

He eschewed using a frame jig, which he felt placed unwanted stress on the thin gauge steel and could cause subsequent warping and hairline cracks.

He preferred to build completely by eye, constantly checking trueness against the hand drawn plans that he custom designed for each client.

When it was time to proceed with the brazing, he turned on his oxyacetylene tanks, and lighting the torch he adjusted the flow of the gases.

He further fine-tuned the combination of oxygen and acetylene to create optimum inner and outer envelopes of flame.

As he began to heat the area where the chainstays were inserted into the bottom bracket, he was disturbed to hear an unusual hissing sound emanating from the area where the gas tanks were standing.

In all his years of brazing, he had never discerned such a sound before…

Irritated, because the bottom bracket had now reached the perfect shade of cherry red to begin filling in the voids with the bronze rod, he pulled back from his work and looked at the tanks and hoses to determine what was causing the discordant sound.

As he turned with torch in hand, he was aghast to hear, and see, the roar of an ignited conflagration, and feel a concussive explosion.

These were the final impressions in the fading conscious of The Tailor…

CHAPTER ONE

Racing bicycles are the epitome of efficient cycling design.
Elegantly simple and highly responsive, they provide one of the most perfect synergies of human and machine.

Despite ongoing marketing hype through the years about the newest and greatest innovations, other than the introduction of modern lightweight manmade materials such as carbon fiber, and the advent of electronic shifting, the technology of the bicycle has not changed significantly since the 1940s.

Many aficionados of bicycle component design erroneously believe that inventions such as cassette hubs, multi-speed derailleurs and freewheels, lightweight aluminum alloy components, sealed bearings, and index shifting, were all new developments from the 1960s-1980s.

However, as the result of aeronautical engineering and metallurgical innovations during World War II, beautifully crafted examples of these parts from Britain and France were available in limited quantities to those who could afford them from the late 1930s.

Some of these designs were copied, embellished, and rebranded by unscrupulous opportunists, before patent laws in Europe began to be effectual and enforced in the early 1960s.

Also, during this time period, famed French craftsmen began to use aluminum to make elegant lightweight touring frames.

Throughout western Europe, track racing frames made from thin wall butted steel alloy tubing of varying thicknesses, initially developed for use in airplane frames, provided the basis for complete bikes that were as light as 16 pounds.

Just as with the evolution of the automobile, competitive racing provided the catalyst for ongoing bicycle development and enhancements.

Six-day races started in Britain in 1878. They were initially run 24 hours a day and were limited to six days in a row, as there was no racing on Sundays due to religious traditions.

Track racing offered several advantages compared to road racing, for both participants and sponsors.

Early roadways were generally in poor condition, causing flat tires, mechanical failures and accidents.

Other than at race starts and finishes, the long routes did not generally lend themselves to spectator viewing, and promoters were not able to sell tickets to watchers.

Whereas, track races were held in enclosed spaces and could be organized at indoor venues, averting the possibility of inclement weather being a deterrent.

These events proved to be quite lucrative for the organizers.

The six-day races were held on steeply canted oval tracks constructed with wooden boards which provided opportunities to increase speed as a rider descended from the upper edge toward the lower portion of the track.

This design also made it less likely that a rider could inadvertently catch the edge of a pedal against the track surface while leaning into the turns.

There were no brakes on these track racing bicycles.

They were single speed and used a fixed gear that constantly turned in concert with the motion of the wheels.

The rider could not coast by stopping the rotation of the pedals and crankarms as the wheels continued to turn, as one could on a road bicycle outfitted with a freewheel.

Slowing down was accomplished by applying the power of the rider's legs against the forward motion, and by using the friction from a glove with wooden blocks sewn into the palm, manually applied on both sides of the front wheel rim.

In America during the late 1800s, the safety bicycle design with two equally sized wheels, had replaced the much harder-to-ride high-wheeler, and interest in cycling as a spectator sport boomed across a broad demographic.

Bicycles provided inexpensive transportation for the working class and cycling gained popularity as a leisure activity with wealthy vacationers in Palm Beach and other high-end resort destinations.

Famous competitors in early U.S. bicycle races included two men from Indiana.

Marshall Walter Biggs (Major) Taylor set many world records.

He was the first black man to become a world champion in bicycle racing, as well as only the second black man to win a world championship in any sporting discipline.

Consummate promoter Carl Graham Fisher owned a bicycle shop with his brothers, and he was notably successful as a racer.

Later, he segued his *need for speed* into auto racing, and he was a winning driver.

He went on to co-found the Indianapolis 500 motor race, known as the Brickyard 500- so named because the racetrack was paved with bricks after the initial surface disastrously deteriorated during the inaugural race.

He also put together a consortium of automotive manufacturers and dealerships to invest in privately building the cross-country Lincoln Highway, and the Dixie Highway, before President Eisenhower initiated the government funded National Highway System.

Though primarily intended to improve automobile transportation, the expanded roadway system, which used better materials that resulted in smoother and more reliable roads, was also beneficial to bicycling.

But arguably Fisher's greatest business achievement was as the real estate developer who created Miami Beach.

The first six-day race was held at Madison Square Garden in 1891. Those competitions became known as *Madisons*.

Participants were originally solo riders. This changed to teams of two in 1898 when the races became limited to only twelve hours straight per rider due to safety concerns.

These competitions were so onerous that Major Taylor only competed once in a six-day race because he decided that the arduous punishment was too much to endure.

Most of the cyclists who participated in the six-day races came from very modest means.

As successful athletes they became famous and were treated like movie stars.

In addition to lucrative rewards for successful racers from the sponsors, special cash prizes called *primes* were provided by affluent spectators.

In those days, every major city had a *velodrome*, and track bicycle racing was the number one spectator sport in the United States.

However, in America, public interest in bicycles and racing has historically been sporadic and cyclical, and bicycles fell out of favor at the outset of the First World War.

CHAPTER TWO

Appreciation for cycling in Europe has always been much more consistent than in America.

Historically, the European nations have been great cycling rivals. Especially, just prior to, and after World War II.

Successful competition in athletics, including cycling, was perceived to be prestigious for a country's image, as well as good publicity for the sponsors.

The French *Paris-Roubaix* road race, which was organized by the sports newspaper- *Le Velo*, was first held in 1896.

The world's most famous bicycle race- the *Tour-de-France*, began in 1903.

In Britain, point-to-point, time trial, and six-day races were exceedingly popular; given the confines of their island nation, they lacked sufficient geography to host a major long-distance race on the scale of the *Tour-de-France*.

In Italy, the *Giro-di-Lombardia* was first held in 1905. The *Milan-San Remo* race began in 1907.

These two famed races were considered the Italian Classics.

The most challenging Italian bicycle race- the *Giro d'Italia*—inspired by the *Tour-de-France* and intended to rival it—was first run in 1909.

The Spanish *Vuelta-a-Espana* was a relative latecomer and did not begin until 1935.

CHAPTER THREE

There is a common misperception that the use of performance enhancing drugs in bicycle racing is a modern phenomenon.

But from the very first six-day races, riders routinely used nitroglycerine and cocaine to enhance performance, and strychnine to tighten tired muscles.

In the late 1800s, opiates such as tincture of laudanum were widely administered throughout the populace to treat a variety of maladies- in both the United States, and in Europe- and abuse became endemic.

There was a long history of drug usage in the early 1900s European road races.

Competitive cyclists routinely used opiates as pain relievers, and to promote sleep in between race stages.

Assistants who administered these drugs were

called *soigneurs*.

The use of cocaine eyedrops and amphetamines to stay alert, and alcohol and ether to dull pain, were allowed.

Ether was routinely carried in a small bottle called a *topette*.

Under the Harrison Act, opiates, and cocaine, which had previously been fashionable in Europe as snuff for aristocrats, were banned as illegal substances in the United States in 1914 at the start of World War I.

But the use of these drugs continued in Europe, and during the First World War cocaine was given to British troops in the form of forced march tablets.

Up until the 1940s, doping in sports to enhance performance and stamina was an accepted practice.

During World War II, amphetamines and methamphetamines were used extensively, by both the Allied and the Axis forces, for their stimulant and performance-enhancing effects.

In the post-war 1950s, despite being illegal, cocaine became popular again with the rich and famous.

Opioids were still openly used in cycling in the early 1960s, until performance-enhancing drugs for athletic competitions were officially banned in France in 1965.

When amphetamines were made illegal in 1970, criminals began synthesizing them in clandestine labs and sold them on the black market.

In the ever-evolving quest for competitive advantages, athletes also began to use cortisone and other steroids.

CHAPTER FOUR

Gino Fausto was born on a small farm outside of *Casale Monferrato*, between the villages of Asti and Alba, in the *Piemonte* region of Italy (Piedmont).

As a boy, he was thrilled to watch the *Giro d'Italia* race as it passed through the city of *Torino* (Turin).

When Fausto's family moved to *Firenze* (Florence) in Tuscany, to take advantage of a better employment opportunity for his father, who was a winemaker, Fausto met Ernesto Sante.

Fausto was too poor to afford a racing bicycle, so he worked in Sante's shop in exchange for parts and a frame, that he built up in his spare time.

He upgraded the quality of the components whenever he was able to do so.

With Sante's help and coaching, he eventually gained fame as a successful racer, culminating in wins at the prestigious *Milan-San Remo*, *Giro d'Italia*, and *Tour-de-France* races.

He was pictured several times in the *La Gazzetta-dello-Sport* newspaper wearing the *Giro* race leader's *maglia rosa*, pink jersey.

The jersey was so named because the newspaper (*La Gazzetta*) was the race sponsor, and they printed on pink paper.

This association of a vivid jersey color identifying a preeminent rider, and referencing a sponsoring publication, had been brazenly adopted from the *Tour-de-France* yellow jersey, which was created in 1919 because it was the color of the paper used to print- *L'Auto*, which was later renamed- *L'Equipe*.

At the outset of the Second World War, Fausto was conscripted into the Italian army, and he became a messenger.

But his sympathies lay elsewhere, and he covertly helped Jewish refugees by hiding counterfeit identity documents in his bicycle frame.

As a competitive racer, Fausto already had extensive experience with drug use to offset fatigue and stay alert.

For his exhaustive messenger duties, he received a constant supply of drugs from his army doctor to aid him.

As a clandestine agent of the resistance, he was used to a life of secrecy. Though he hid it well, he became helplessly addicted...

CHAPTER FIVE

When most people hear about organized crime in Italy, they tend to think of the Sicilian Mafia, or *Cosa Nostra*, which is the oldest crime cartel in Italy.

But there are several similar powerful crime syndicates that originate from other southern Italian regions.

The Neapolitan *Camorra*, from Campania, was formed in the mid-1800s as a prison gang. Their members are known as *camorristi*.

Historically, narcotics and sex-trafficking provided significant revenue streams for the *Camorra*, but they profited even more from public-sector fraud, construction contracts, waste management, blackmail, counterfeited products, money laundering and contraband cigarettes.

They were the first of the Italian organized crime mobs to expand their activities into France.

Unlike the Sicilian Mafia, which has a clear hierarchy, the *Camorra's* organization and activities are much less centralized, and as such, are harder for law enforcement to identify and combat. Their system of operation is known as *O Sistema.*

In Puglia, an offshoot splinter group of the *Camorra* is known as the *Nuova Sacra Corona,* or *Sacra Corona Unita.*

In Calabria, the gang known as the *Ndrangheta* came to prominence in the 1860s and 1870s.

They became Italy's largest, richest and most powerful organized crime syndicate.

Like the *Camorra*, they were involved in extortion and blackmail, and they expanded into kidnapping, drug smuggling, money laundering and contraband cigarettes.

They also became involved in boxing and other sports- including cycling, as a method to launder money, and to expand the outlets for their narcotics business.

The *Ndrangheta* was the first Italian crime syndicate to build a presence in northern Italy in the 1950s.

In the immediate aftermath of the Second World War, Italy suffered a lack of coherent political organization, and the various organized crime groups took full advantage of the opportunity to consolidate their power, and branch out into other illicit business endeavors.

Most people in Europe at that time could not afford cars, motorcycles, or motorized scooters, so cycling and walking were their only viable transportation options, and bicycle sales saw strong growth.

However, in the 1950s, as economies recovered, and motorized transportation became more available and affordable, bicycles were no longer the preferred mode of transportation.

Up until the early 1950s, bicycle manufacturers were the sole sponsors of the *Giro d'Italia* but beginning in 1954 large companies from other industries and businesses, who perceived a benefit to promoting their brands through the popularity of the *Giro*, became significant underwriters.

Because of the dramatic decline in bicycle sales, many of the traditional bicycle brands could no longer afford the significant expense of subsidizing a racing team.

A full year prior to this grudgingly sanctioned change to the financial support infrastructure of the *Giro*, in 1953, under the guise of sponsorship, the *Ndrangheta* moved into professional bicycle racing to facilitate increasing their very profitable drug sales to the competing athletes.

To conform with the established practice of only bicycle manufacturers sending teams to the *Giro*, through the Ferraro bakeries and cheese factories that they owned near the coastal Calabrian town of Zambrone, just north of Tropea, the *Ndrangheta* purchased a failing bicycle parts manufacturing business in the town of Merate in *Lombardia* (Lombardy).

The business had recently suffered crippling financial losses due to intense competition from its rival- the Campagnolo company.

They used this company, rebranded under the

Ferraro name, to sponsor a race team.

The star racer of the team was named Giovanni Ferraro.

His mission was to infiltrate the highest echelons of bicycle racing, sell banned drugs to the racers, and strongarm the competition to assure success for *Cicli Ferraro*...

CHAPTER SIX

In the early days of road racing, even the most prestigious large races, had individual, or small private team participants.

But as the sport evolved, national and corporate sponsorships became involved. Teams by country began in 1930.

In Italy, no races were held during World War I. But scaled-down versions of the *Giro* continued for the first years of World War II.

However, when Benito Mussolini was deposed in 1943, all racing in Italy stopped until 1946.

When racing resumed, these exciting sports events drew large crowds, and they were a welcome respite for a war weary world.

Racers from other countries were permitted to compete in the *Giro*, but they raced for teams under the auspices of Italian bicycle manufacturers.

In both 1949 and 1952, at the insistence of the

Italian government, which was anxious to restore some international prestige, Gino Fausto competed in the *Tour-de-France* in addition to racing in the *Giro*.

To the delight of the politicians, and with great acclaim, he was the *vincitore* (winner) of all four races!

But in 1950, for the first time a non-Italian racer won the *Giro*...

CHAPTER SEVEN

Gentullio (Tullio) Campagnolo was from *Vicenza* (Venice) in the Veneto.

He was an amateur racer who became a successful inventor and manufacturer of beautifully finished proprietary high-end bicycle components.

In 1933 he started his eponymous company. He fabricated prototypes in the back of his father's hardware store, and he engaged the *Fratelli Brivio* (F.B.) factory, of Brescia, as a subcontractor to manufacture parts for commercial production.

Legend has it that while racing over the snowy Croce D'Aune pass in the Dolomite mountains, Tullio lost the race due to not being able to loosen the frozen wingnuts on the axle of his rear wheel hub.

He was unable to reverse the wheel and manually move the chain to the larger gear sprocket, on the other side, which he needed to accomplish to facilitate a better ratio for easier peddling up the steep mountain.

As the story goes, this prompted his subsequent invention and patenting of a quick release cam-operated mechanism.

However, the reality is that several French companies made similar products that pre-dated Campagnolo's initial production.

Similarly, Campagnolo was also purported to be the inventor of the parallelogram rear derailleur.

But both Nivex and JIC had previously produced small quantities of similar shifting mechanisms.

Though not the original inventor of these designs, as claimed by the company's marketing, Campagnolo did a commendable job of copying, adapting, and improving upon other manufacturers' concepts.

He developed complete *gruppos* (interrelated sets of components), and skillfully promoted them through racer sponsorships, where the riders were required to only use his products, thereby blocking his competitors from the significant exposure and publicity generated from the races, which influenced consumer purchases.

Previously, racers chose individual components for their bicycles, *ad hoc*, from multiple specialty brands.

By 1948 Campagnolo was manufacturing many of his own components, and he had facilities in Cognin, France and in Vincenza, Italy.

F.B. still made hubs for Campagnolo, and they shared the Cognin facility to service the French market, because of restrictive import tariffs at the time.

After World War II Tullio became close friends with frame maker Ernesto Sante, and with Gino Fausto's father- Enrico.

They were all Christian Democrats, the political party that held the majority of the Italian Parliament in 1953, and which was the current ruling faction.

While they originally met each other because of their political beliefs and a shared love of cycling, Tullio became an ardent fan of the Tuscan *Chianti Classico* red wines that Enrico crafted- especially the aged *Riservas*.

During dinners together, they would often imbibe Enrico's wines, which they felt were superior to the *Valpolicella* and *Bardolino* red wines produced near where Tulio lived.

However, they would invariably finish the meal with a delicious *Monte Veronese* cheese—made by Tullio's cousin in the Lessini mountains of northern Verona—and a glass, or two, of rare *Amarone* wine that Tullio had acquired from a family friend in exchange for bicycle parts.

They all agreed that this concentrated wine made from grapes dried in the sun on straw mats was one of Italy's greatest wines.

These shared vinous experiences inspired Tullio, to subsequently design and manufacture a patented *Cavitappi* corkscrew in 1966.

When Gino resumed his racing career after the war, Campagnolo sponsored him with free parts for his bicycles.

In 1950 Fausto won the famed *Paris-Roubaix* race using a Campagnolo *una leva*, or single lever derailleur, that was subsequently renamed *Paris-Roubaix* in honor of his win.

As of 1952 all Campagnolo components were made in-house, and they no longer used F.B. for any production.

In that year Fausto won the *Giro d'Italia* and the *Tour-de-France* using Campagnolo *Gran Sport Extra* derailleurs.

CHAPTER EIGHT

The route of the 1953 *Giro d'Italia*, which covered four thousand thirty-five *kilometres*, was seventy-one *kilometres* longer than the previous year's competition which Fausto had won.

The race took place over twenty-one days. Sixteen teams competed. Each consisting of seven riders.

Of the one hundred and twelve starters, seventy-two participants finished the race.

1953 was the first year for live television coverage for some of the stage finishes.

Prior to that, only portions of previous races had been filmed for later broadcast.

In addition to the usual mountain stage in the Dolomites, with the steep Misurina, Falzarego, Pordoi and Sella passes, the highlight climbing stage of the 1953 *Giro* was the first crossing of the daunting Stelvio Pass, which encompassed forty-eight treacherous switchbacks.

The race began in *Milano* (Milan) in the *Lombardia* (Lombardy) region and proceeded to the Adriatic coast of Italy.

There was a large crowd of spectators at the start, who were eager to see their favorite riders and cheer on the competitors.

The racers wore colorful wool jerseys proudly proclaiming their team affiliations, and chamois padded wool cycling shorts.

They all sported freshly shaved legs, not for any perceived aerodynamic improvement, but to avoid having hair in the scabs from the inevitable road rash abrasions.

Most riders had small over-the-shoulder cycling bags, called *musettes*, for holding food and tools, which also prominently featured the logos of their bicycle brand and team sponsor.

Water bottles, called *bidons*, were made of thin gauge aluminum, and were stoppered with natural corks.

Open finger padded cycling gloves, made of pigskin leather and string-backed woven cotton, aided grip, but provided only minimal shock absorption.

Cycling shoes, in those days were made of thin leather, with numerous holes for breathability and lightness.

Metal cleats, designed to straddle the pedal flanges, were hand-fitted and hammered into the bottoms of the shoes by cobblers.

Adjustable leather straps were threaded through the pedals and toeclips, and securely held the rider's foot in place to maximize torque and efficiency.

However, this made it difficult for the rider to quickly extricate his foot in a panic situation.

Most competitors used handmade high pressure, tubular tires known as *sewups*, which were glued to a flangeless wheel rim.

These were preferable to clincher tires, which were held within the hooked profile of a clincher rim by the internal air pressure, with a thick rubber, or metal bead on the inner circumference of the tire.

Even when *sewup* tires went flat, since they were glued to the rim, they tended to stay on it, cover the metal edges, and still provide a modicum of traction.

Since they did not have a rigid bead like a clincher tire, *sewups* could be folded and were easier to carry.

Riders could bring spare *sewups* in their *musettes* or slung across their back.

Most racers rode with no protective headgear. Some wore the peaked short-billed cotton caps known as *casquettes*, more to further promote their team logo and help soak up sweat, than because of any actual protection from the elements or adversity that they afforded.

A few more prudent participants used padded leather hairnets, even though in practice they only provided minimal crash protection.

Other than two riders prematurely dropping out of the race, the first stage finished uneventfully at Abano Terme in the Veneto, or Venetia region.

CHAPTER NINE

There is a longstanding inherit distrust and antipathy between northern and southern Italians- a legacy from the time of separate city-states, and foreign government intrusions and alliances.

This animosity is also a reflection of the perceived superior culture and industrialized wealth in the north, versus the more agricultural rural lifestyle and extensive poverty in the south.

In the 1950s per capita income in the southern part of the country was half that of northern Italy.

Given that history, an epic battle between Team Sante and Team Ferraro was looming.

The sponsor rivalry between the Campagnolo and Ferraro manufacturing brands also set the tone for aggressive competition between the two teams in the *Giro*.

With his mentor Sante so recently deceased,

Fausto had become increasingly dependent on Campagnolo to help guide his team and prepare their strategy.

To Campagnolo, the former racer, Fausto had become like an adopted son.

Perhaps he saw in Gino a reminder of himself from years gone by.

Tullio had contacts with the French racers who were participating in the *Giro*.

These riders would be racing under the auspices of an Italian team that used his components, and he had also previously sponsored them in France because of his former factory in Cognin, which he had just recently closed.

He arranged for them to collaborate with Team Sante, and to help protect and pace Fausto during the race.

But unbeknownst to Fausto and Campagnolo, Ferraro had already made a deal with his counterparts in the *Camorra*, who had expanded their criminal activities into France.

In exchange for concessions in the lucrative cigarette smuggling business they had secretly agreed to help Ferraro win the race.

They would be especially active during the stage that would pass through their home region *Napoli* (Naples), and they would subvert to their cause the French racers, who were dependent on them for performance enhancing drugs, which was a much more compelling inducement then what Campagnolo had offered...

CHAPTER TEN

The second stage of the *Giro* went from Abano Terme to Rimini in Emilia-Romagna.

It featured the first major ascent of the race, at San Marino.

As the riders departed, Fausto caught a quick glimpse of Ferraro staring at him intently, with a knowing look, like a master card player who confidently held the winning hand...

A foreboding sensation of impending trouble left Fausto with an uneasy feeling...

Fausto was using the third iteration newest version of the Campagnolo *Gran Sport* derailleurs, which facilitated the use of a larger freewheel, and allowed for gear ratios that made riding up steep slopes easier.

However, this required using the friction shifters with additional finesse.

He would have to carefully fine-tune the

alignment of the increased chain line between freewheel and crank chainrings, to avoid chain slippage, or the chain getting wedged between the chainrings, or falling off entirely.

At some points in a long race, riders may be stretched out far from each other along the route.

When bunched together, and riding in a pack known as a *peloton*, riders often draft only *centimetres* off the rear wheel of the bicycle in front of them to take advantage of the aerodynamic effect, with no margin for error.

If wheels touch, in a split second an entire line of riders can collide into each other, in a domino effect chain reaction, with disastrous results.

An assisting team rider, who helps set the pace and provide motivation for the squad leader, is called a *domestique* (in French), or *gregario* (in Italian).

Like many cyclists in those times, as part of his preparations before beginning a long ride, Fausto would habitually apply a soothing cream to the chamois pad inside his wool cycling shorts to help reduce friction and avoid irritation and saddle sores.

When they began the approach to San Marino, Fausto's *gregario*- Mauro, led him out in a breakaway from the *peloton*.

As they increased their pace, Fausto began to breathe more heavily and sweat profusely.

He noticed a slight tingling sensation in his lower extremities, which, over time became more bothersome.

As the *kilometres* went by, his skin in the

affected areas began to itch unbearably.

The condition worsened, and it took all his concentration to try and ignore the intense compulsion to scratch the effected skin, remain focused on his pace, and stay on Mauro's wheel.

As Fausto tried to contend with this increasingly excruciating distraction, he lost his peddling rhythm, and Mauro started to pull away from him.

With his *gregario* no longer blocking the wind for him and providing an aerodynamic advantage, he lost more speed.

He failed to notice that Ferraro and his teammates were on the attack, and that they had closed in on him.

As they neared the crest of San Marino, Ferraro triumphantly passed Fausto, flicking his hand under his chin in a gesture of contempt.

Mauro dropped back to reconnect with Fausto, but Ferraro was reputed to be fearless in fast descents, and so he proved after crossing over San Marino.

Though Fausto rallied and fought through his agony until the finish, he never caught Ferraro, who won the stage.

As he crossed the line, Ferraro jubilantly raised his arms and threw air kisses to pretty girls in the crowd.

Meanwhile, the *tifosi* (fans), who had no affection for southerners, jeered at him as the television cameras filmed his antics.

That evening, belated relief for Fausto came in the form of imbibing some potent local brandy, known as *grappa*, and by applying a powerful topical antihistamine to his abraded rashes.

Together, these measures helped to alleviate the severe irritation.

As he drifted into an uneasy sleep, Fausto wondered what could have caused his acute discomfort...

Had someone surreptitiously tampered with the balm he used on the chamois in his shorts?

CHAPTER ELEVEN

The third stage of the race went from Rimini to San Benedetto-del-Tronto in Marche along the Adriatic Sea.

Fausto felt weary and drained most of the day from the after-effects of his mysterious malady, and to his team's consternation, and despite their efforts to motivate him, he did not perform well, finishing in mid-pack.

However, as they rode along the seaside he found the inhalation of the briny tang of the fresh sea air restorative, and he felt much better that evening.

Ferraro seemed satisfied to bask in the glory of his previous win, and he did not push the pace, content to finish several minutes behind the stage winner.

That night, as Campagnolo was preparing Fausto's bicycle, and those of his squad for the next day, he fixated on formulating a strategy to regain precious time.

He repacked the freewheels on the bicycles using some of his proprietary grease to lubricate them, instead of using oil.

With this technique, the palls would be silent when they coasted, instead of clicking when they fell into place, thus allowing his riders to stealthily attack and sneak up on their rivals...

CHAPTER TWELVE

J ust prior to the outset of stage four, Campagnolo huddled with Fausto and his team, and he explained his plan.

The racers headed out from San Benedetto-del-Tronto, en route to Roccaraso in Abruzzo. This stage featured an ascent at Cinque Miglia.

Fausto and his teammates spent the first part of the race mid-pack, well behind Ferraro and his team, moving along at a medium pace, while they passed water bottles and smoked strong cigarettes—their heartbeats accelerated by the strong nicotine.

As the race neared Cinque Miglia, Fausto's group, along with several other riders began to increase their pace and move up.

As they chased down riders in front of them, they were almost undone when a little girl ran out into the road to fetch a *musette* that a rider had dropped.

The pack had to violently swerve to avoid her, almost causing several accidents. A Swiss rider was unable to avoid crashing into her.

Thankfully, she was not seriously hurt, but the rider went down hard and was knocked senseless, and his bicycle was a useless tangled mess...

A teammate stayed behind to help his fallen captain, and to arrange a replacement bicycle, as Fausto's squad continued their relentless pursuit.

As Fausto's group approached the rise in incline toward Cinque Mille, they saw that Ferraro was engrossed in conversation with his *gregario*, and that he had let his vigilance wane.

With his wind-tousled hair, a spare *sewup* tire slung across his shoulder like a bandolier of rifle cartridges, and a filter-less cigarette casually drooping from his mouth, Ferraro looked nonchalant.

He slowed for a moment to pass a water bottle to his teammate, unaware of the progress of his nemesis.

Mauro and Fausto, taking turns drafting each other, and with Campagnolo's specially prepared freewheels, silently attacked Ferraro and his men.

Con brio, they blew by them like a freight train under full steam, and they continued up to the summit.

Ferraro had proved that he was exceedingly fast in the descents, but on the ascent, he was incapable of challenging Fausto who was a consummate climber.

Fausto triumphantly won the day, but Ferraro

remained the overall race leader.

Due to a valiant effort by his *gregario*, who set a brisk pace and brought him along for twenty *kilometres*, the Swiss competitor, bloodied and bandaged, managed to complete the stage and remain in the race...

CHAPTER THIRTEEN

T he next morning the racers left Roccaraso, and headed to *Napoli* (Naples) in Campania—home region of the *Cammora*, who had arranged a warm welcome for Fausto and his team...

Crowd control at bicycle races was often lax. It was not unusual for partisan fans to spit on cyclists from rival teams or throw garbage at them.

When the racers entered the outskirts of *Napoli*, spectators cheered on the Ferraro team, but they belligerently heckled and physically hindered the other racers.

They were delighted at the opportunity to disparage the northern Italian and foreign athletes, while officials and politicians who had been paid off by the *Cammora* turned a blind eye.

Navigating narrow streets was made more difficult by having to steer around mailboxes and other obstructions that protruded from some of the walls.

Unbeknownst to most racing fans, competitive cycling is often an aggressive contact sport, with elbows, shoulders, and hips used to impede and delay rivals, and cause crashes.

As a pack of riders, including Fausto and several members of team Sante rounded a corner, Mauro was viciously bumped into a mailbox by an unseen opponent.

The force of the contact swept his arms aside and caught him squarely in his ribs, instantly knocking all the air from his lungs as he gasped in intense pain.

With his feet securely cleated to his pedals, his torso jackknifed over the mailbox, while his legs and bicycle attempted to continue the forward momentum.

Fausto looked back to see what had caused the loud noise, and in surreal slow motion he saw Mauro, still attached to his bicycle, lean backwards, and then fall over onto his side, with his head slamming into the cobblestones with a loud sickening crack…

CHAPTER FOURTEEN

F
austo dismounted. Trying not to slip and fall as his metal cleats slid on the pavement, he ran to Mauro, calling for his compatriots to find a doctor!

As he examined Mauro, he was relieved to see that he was conscious and apparently only dazed.

His friend's skull must be very thick to absorb such punishment!

There was a large nasty lump on his head, but he seemed coherent, and with a weak smile he told Fausto that his ribs felt broken.

Fausto looked up to see if anyone had found medical assistance, and he felt reassured to see his teammate Guido approaching with a race doctor.

Guido assured him that he would make sure that Mauro was well taken care of, and he urged Fausto to rejoin the race.

Fausto well knew that his responsibility to his

team, and his commitment to his sponsor-Campagnolo, was an oath not lightly taken.

With a grim expression, he told the doctor to be sure to check for signs of shock and other latent trauma.

He nodded to Guido as he mounted his bicycle and sprinted away.

His seething sentiment—to catch and defeat whoever was the perpetrator of this immoral act!

CHAPTER FIFTEEN

The hospital had reported that Mauro was recovering, but he was out of commission for the remainder of the race.

After an uneasy night for team Sante, there was a flurry of activity the next morning as everyone scrambled to be ready for the next leg of the race, which ran from *Napoli* to *Roma* (Rome).

When Fausto and his squad assembled at the starting line, Team Ferraro lined up next to them.

Professional cycling could be ruthless. While Fausto could not be sure who the malefactor was that had caused Mauro's accident, he suspected that Team Ferraro, and their haughty leader was responsible.

With an insouciant expression, Ferraro said *sotto voce* to Fausto, "Your friend's accident, was unfortunate. We have a saying in Calabria—*tirano-a-campa!* (live day-to-day)."

His expression as the race began, was unreadable, but his intention was clearly a warning...

Thirty *kilometres* into the two hundred and eight-five *kilometres* route for the day, the team Sante bikes began to break down...

CHAPTER SIXTEEN

Campagnolo was a seasoned racing veteran, both as a former participant, and as a major sponsor of elite competitors.

Through his vast experience with component design and production, he was able to quickly problem solve and get Fausto and his team back on the road, in spite of the fact that they had suffered twenty different major breakdowns along the route that day.

While they were not able to improve their position, they managed to finish mid-pack, and they would be able to continue to compete in the remaining stages.

That evening, though disgruntled because of the setbacks, and at the lost time they had suffered, they were thankful that at least none of the remaining team members had been obliged to drop out of the race.

After he and his mechanics had more thoroughly inspected all the equipment, Tullio pulled Gino aside.

"You know I take great pride in the quality and reliability of the parts we produce.

"To have this many significant failures in one day is not normal, and I was deeply concerned that this reflected badly on my reputation, and that you might think me undependable!

"But from our inspections we have determined that some of the components were cleverly sabotaged!

"This must have been done last night while we were all preoccupied about Mauro.

"I take full responsibility for our lapse in vigilance, and you have my word that this will never happen again!"

Fausto assured Campagnolo of his ongoing trust. Each of them more than suspected that Ferraro was the culprit behind this latest ploy to undermine the Sante team, and they agreed that more subterfuge, was likely as the race progressed...

CHAPTER SEVENTEEN

Participating in the 1953 *Giro* were several French riders that Fausto had competed against the previous year in the *Tour-de-France.*

On the stage from *Roma* to Grosseto in Tuscany, about ninety *kilometres* into the route a group of these French riders caught up to Fausto and his squad.

Based on Campagnolo's previous assurances to Fausto that he had convinced the French riders to assist Team Sante, Fausto assumed that they would all now work together to advance their position in the overall field.

For the first several hours that appeared to be the shared plan.

They all switched off, taking the lead in the paceline, then dropping back to let the next rider take his turn, as they rode through the picturesque

Maremma countryside, much of which had formerly been marshland until drained in the 1930s.

As they passed by vineyards, Fausto lamented that he could not send Guido in search of some of the non-indigenous Cabernet Sauvignon grapes for him to taste, which had been planted at the end of the war.

Though the harvest was still several months away, and the grapes had not yet fully ripened, his father had told him that 1953 was shaping up to be an excellent vintage.

Fausto noticed that several of the French riders seemed overly animated and hyped-up, likely due to excessive use of stimulants.

As a habitual drug user himself, he could easily identify the telltale signs.

All seemed to be progressing to plan, until they reached the shoreline of the Tyrrhenian Sea.

They passed a group of waving spectators on a hillside, who proceeded to take pictures with the large camera they had set up on a tripod, overlooking the course.

As the riding order changed, with one of the French riders falling back to let Fausto take his place at the lead, Fausto was startled to hear an alarmed shout from Guido.

Out of the corner of his eye, he saw him veer off the road and bounce over the rough shoulder towards the precipitous edge of the steep slope that descended to the water below.

With alarmed concern, Fausto stopped abruptly, causing the rider behind him to narrowly avoid crashing into him, and the other following riders to swerve to avoid a similar fate.

Fausto watched Guido lay his bike down, and slide into a small stone retaining wall.

Miraculously, Guido was not badly hurt. He loosened the toe straps on his pedals so he could pull his feet free, and yelling profanities, he proceeded to run at one of the French riders and tackle him to the ground.

The other Frenchmen came to the aid of their countryman, and of course, Fausto's teammates joined the fight.

Fausto waded in, pulled the struggling bodies apart, and he demanded to know what had caused the *melee*.

Guido replied that the Frenchman named Pierre had intentionally steered him off the road!

Pierre indigently replied that it had been an accident, caused by his running over a rock, and trying to regain his balance.

Tempers did not abate, and no amicable resolution was attainable, so Fausto admonished the French riders to keep clear of him and his teammates, and they all remounted, and proceeded down the road.

Before putting distance between the two groups, the riders glared at each other, uttered derogatory invectives, and used suggestive insulting hand gestures.

At Guido's insistence, when they arrived in Grosseto Team Sante formally lodged a complaint with the race marshals.

At the inquiry that evening, fortuitously, one of the spectators who was a professional photographer, and had been taking pictures of the race, attended.

He produced a photograph showing three hands steering Guido's handlebars!

The guilty Frenchman—a Corsican, who claimed to be Parisian—was disqualified, and thrown out of the race.

CHAPTER EIGHTEEN

The eighth stage of the *Giro* was the individual time trial, which continued the journey through Tuscany, traveling from Grosseto to Follonica.

Fausto had a blind masseuse, named Blasio, who helped him with his recoveries from over-exertion and accident damage, and kept him fit.

He had provided Fausto with sound advice and had been his confidant for several years.

It was rumored that he also provided recommendations about drug use, and he helped Fausto fine tune and administer the doses that he habitually used.

For the time trial, Blasio had successfully performed his therapeutic massage magic, and Fausto was in fine form.

He finished in third place, a mere eighty-one seconds behind the winner.

CHAPTER NINETEEN

The race continued through the countryside of Tuscany, from Follonica to Pisa.

Fausto and his teammates were effusively cheered on at the start by his father, and a large contingent of employees from the winery where Enrico worked.

In post-war Italy, concerns about a possible communist *coup d'état* had dominated political discourse for several years, until the ascendancy of the Christian Democratic party, whose members were anti-communist and opposed to socialism.

However, the Communist-Socialist alliance remained strong in the central regions of Emilia-Romagna, *Tuscana* (Tuscany) and in Umbria.

Trade unions in Italy were relatively weak until the late 1960s, and they were divided politically into competing federations.

The communists and socialists were in the Italian

General Confederation of Labour.

The Catholic and Christian Democrats were in the Italian Confederation of Workers' Trade Unions, and the moderate Italian Labour Union.

The Christian Democrats had a strong social and religious base with the industrial *bourgeoisie* in the northern regions of Italy, as well as backing from the landowners in the south.

They were supported by the Catholic Church which had excommunicated the communists.

They also had another unlikely ally in organized crime, which viewed the communists and socialists, and their workers' movement, as their enemy.

CHAPTER TWENTY

From Pisa, the race proceeded to Modena in Emilia-Romagna, and this stage included a major ascent at Abetone.

The Russian intelligence agency known as the Committee for State Security, or KGB, was officially established in 1954 after Josef Stalin died in March 1953.

However, its agents, who were drawn primarily from the *Cheka*, the People's Commissariat for State Security (NKGB), as well as the OGPU, NKVD and MGB, were already active in international espionage in the summer of 1953.

In Albania, which was known in those days as the People's Socialist Republic of Albania, their secret police, who were under the direction of the *Sigurimi*—or Directorate of State Security— received training from the KGB, and closely cooperated with them.

In 1949 the governments of the United States and the United Kingdom orchestrated an elaborate covert plot to overthrow Albania's communist government.

They recruited Albanian political exiles and refugees, including some from Italy, to serve as mercenaries in guerrilla units that infiltrated Albania in 1950 and 1952.

Due to compromised intelligence most of them were slaughtered.

Of the rest, those few that avoided capture tried to escape.

In Calabria, there was an indigenous Albanian minority, whose antecedents had fled the Turkish Ottoman conquest of their homeland and settled in southern Italy.

The *Ndrangheta* used some of these expatriate Albanians as merciless enforcers.

One such henchman was Adem Dushku, newly returned from the disastrous coup attempt in Albania.

Whether by luck, cunning, or a fortuitous confluence of both, he had survived.

Before his departure, he had managed to assassinate an officer of the *Sigurimi*. A grim retribution for the killing of his compatriots.

During World War II he had fought for the Italian resistance, and he had been trained as a *sabotatore* (saboteur).

He had been a mercenary for the *Ndrangheta* ever since the war ended, and he was an expert in demolitions and unconventional warfare.

Several weeks before the *Giro*, in a ruthless

effort to undermine the Sante racing team prior to the race, he had rigged Ernesto Sante's shop to explode.

Now, from his vantage point on a bluff overlooking the race route at Abetone, Dushku waited until he could see Fausto and one of his teammates approaching in the distance.

Quickly he scrambled down to the roadside at the end of a steeply descending curve, and he carefully looked in all directions to make sure that there were no spectators nearby.

After opening a small leather sack which had been hanging from his belt, he spread the contents of finely ground glass and small sharp rocks across the pavement.

From his previous commando experience, and his innate guile, Dushku relied on simplistic solutions for his ambushes which were hard to detect.

This sabotage would be certain to cause tire punctures and accidents, and it would likely be attributed to natural causes.

Unbeknownst to Dushku, whose view had been partially obscured by the mountainous terrain, a rival Italian rider had been closing in on Fausto and his teammate.

As they approached the trap that Dushku had set, hoping for a stage victory the other rider attacked, and passed Fausto, who was not inclined to waste precious energy chasing him down since he was not an overall contender.

When the accelerating rider ran over the shards of glass, he was ten *metres* ahead of Fausto.

Both of his tires immediately blew out, causing him to lose control and slide off the road, where he flipped over his bicycle and came to rest in a heap against a rocky outcropping.

Fausto had just enough time to apply his brakes, modulating them so as not to lock up his wheels, and slow sufficiently to avoid the same consequence, although his rear tire went flat.

His colleague was able to stop just short of the debris, and as Fausto attended to his bike, his teammate went to check on the injured rider.

Fausto quickly removed the damaged tire and replaced it with a spare, which he industriously pumped up to seven Bar of pressure (equivalent to 101.5 psi).

Though that high volume of air made the tire less pliable, and it would transmit more vibration and shock, and this technique might increase the chance for another blowout, it would also help keep the tire adhered to the rim even though the glue had not yet fully dried and lessen the possibility that it could roll off during high-speed cornering maneuvers.

Their competitor indicated that he was winded, but would be okay, and that they should resume the race.

He borrowed a spare from Fausto's compatriot, changed both of his tires, and they all remounted and continued in the descent from the pass.

Hidden in his elevated position nestled in the rocks above them, Dushku watched in disbelief as they continued down the road.

He was impressed with the tenacity of these athletes. They were worthy adversaries!

CHAPTER TWENTY-ONE

Prior to the start of the team time trial the next morning at the Modena *Autodrome*, Fausto was burned out from the intense exertion and stress at Abetone, and he was still jittery from the after-effects of taking too many amphetamines-with a perpetually dry mouth and symptoms of hypothermia.

However, he felt much better after imbibing some rare local balsamic vinegar that Blasio had given him—made from the must of *Trebbiano* grapes that had been aged in wood barrels for twelve years—and reputed to have healthful benefits, including aiding digestion and managing blood sugar.

64

CHAPTER TWENTY-TWO

From Modena, the race headed to *Genova* (Genoa) in Liguria.

As a group of riders including Fausto's squad approached the seaside of the Italian Riviera, they were joined by the Frenchmen who were intent on getting even for the ousting of their teammate.

Skillfully, the French riders moved up through the *peloton*, situated themselves around Fausto, and boxed him in so that he was unable to maneuver or break away.

When disaster struck, Fausto miscalculated. Without warning, two of the Frenchmen in front of him jammed on their brakes. Fausto zigged, when he should have zagged...

Almost simultaneously as he ran into the back of one of their bicycles, two of his teammates crashed into him.

The result was a mass accident, with more bikes

and riders falling, and eventually coming to a halt strewn across the roadway.

Fausto was badly scraped along the arm he had used, to try and cushion his fall, with similar damage along his back, but thanks to luck and his quick reflexes, he was otherwise unscathed.

By the time he had assessed the damage and righted himself, the Frenchmen had already remounted and ridden off down the road.

As Fausto looked over at his teammates, he could sense that their thoughts were aligned.

There was an unspoken agreement that at the earliest opportunity they would exact their revenge on these *facia-di-merda* Frenchmen!

CHAPTER TWENTY-THREE

The thirteenth stage of the race continued through Liguria from *Genova* to Bordighera.

Fausto had been raised a devout Catholic. Though lapsed in his faith, and publicly criticized and admonished by the church for an affair with a married woman, he still remembered his traditional upbringing, and he was superstitious about the unlucky symbolism of the thirteenth stage...

He awoke at dawn with feelings of apprehension and foreboding...

His mistress, Giulia, who knew of his concerns, had bravely publicly kissed him at the start of the stage, despite the repressive environment for women in 1950s Italy, and she had pressed a small wooden cross into his hand.

In response, an unscrupulous journalist wrote about her in the local newspaper that day to say, "the harsh, unforgiving morning light, revealed a former beauty, who, rumor had it, had passed through many hands..."

As Fausto climbed toward the *Passo-del-Turchino* (Turchino Pass), with a chill that was not a result of the frigid temperature he remembered the *Strage-del-Turchino* (Turchino massacre) during World War II, in which German soldiers had mercilessly murdered innocent civilians in retaliation for an attack by Fausto's colleagues in the Italian resistance.

The cocaine he had sniffed before departing did little to allay his angst and paranoia, but despite his misgivings he made good time, and he finished the day undamaged.

CHAPTER TWENTY-FOUR

The fourteenth stage of the Giro, from Bordighera into *Piemonte* (Piedmont), finished in the city of *Torino* (Turin), and was uneventful.

Fausto crossed the line after the first ten finishers, but he remained in second place overall.

That evening, he and his team carbo-loaded to restore energy by feasting on a delicious local Piemontese recipe of *gnocchi gratin*.

It was prepared by friends from the nearby town of Monferrato where he had grown up.

The small handmade potato dumplings were stuffed with vegetables, including olives, which were rarely cultivated this far north, and baked with a topping of *Fontina* cheese sauce and breadcrumbs, paired with an aged *Barbera* that his father had made at the winery where he had formerly worked.

The rich repast and full-bodied red wine were

very therapeutic, and they all slept soundly that night for the first time since the race had begun.

CHAPTER TWENTY-FIVE

From *Torino*, the racers headed to San Pellegrino Terme in Bergamo, *Lombardia* (Lombardy).

All that day, Fausto was distracted, and he had difficulty focusing on the task at hand.

As he gazed out at the pastoral scenery, his thoughts increasingly turned to Giulia.

He further preoccupied his mind by sending Guido to purloin *Nebbiolo* grapes, known locally as *Spanna*, from a *Gattinara* vineyard, as they traversed past it, so he could taste them.

Though Guido cajoled him throughout the day to pick up the pace, he was unsuccessful.

Nevertheless, Fausto remained in second place overall, but he did not add to his *palmares* (list of winning races) that day, with many riders finishing ahead of him.

CHAPTER TWENTY-SIX

From San Pellegrino Terme, the race proceeded to the town of Riva-del-Garda, situated on the north shore of the majestic *Lago-de-Garda* (Lake Garda) in Trentino-Alto-Adige, also known as the *Sudtyrol* (South Tyrol).

Fausto perpetuated his practice of pilfering from local vineyards, this time with white *Trebbiano* grapes.

Dushku was waiting for Fausto at the Tonale ascent.

His scheme was to place a thin wire across the road, hidden in a layer of dirt that he would pull just as Fausto's front wheel reached it.

Fausto would never see it, and the force of the contact would break the wire, which would likely remain unseen in the aftermath of the crash.

But when he went to hide at the roadside, his plan was thwarted when he unexpectedly encountered a large group of spectators.

He was vexed not to be able to enact his strategy, and he glowered in frustration as he watched Fausto ride by, but this was only a temporary setback.

Dushku, was a meticulous tactician, and he had already formulated other snares along the route, in preparation against just such a possibility...

CHAPTER TWENTY-SEVEN

From Riva-del-Garda, the seemingly relentless punishing pace continued to *Vicenza* (Venice) in *Venetia* (Veneto).

At the end of World War II, the nearby seaport of Trieste, which had been held by the Nazis until their surrender, was taken over by the Yugoslavs.

Subsequently, it became an independent city state under the protection of the United Nations, as the Free Territory of Trieste.

Under their occupation in 1944, the Germans had built the only concentration camp and crematorium on Italian soil, just outside of Trieste at the Risiera-di-San Sabba.

Later that year, in one air raid on Trieste, forty planes from the American Air Force dropped a hundred tons of bombs on the adjacent oil refineries, resulting in damage and destruction to almost one thousand buildings, with four hundred and sixty-three fatalities.

In 1954, parts of this territory were returned to Italian rule, and the city of Trieste was restored as the capitol of the Friuli-Venezia-Giulia region, with the remainder of the contested area ceded to Yugoslavia.

But during the 1953 *Giro*, Trieste was still foreign soil, and an ideal location from which to launch an operation by a covert force.

While most of the local inhabitants were preoccupied with the approaching race, a *Sigurimi* assassin infiltrated *Vicenza*, with the mission to seek reprisal for the recent killing of their senior officer.

Due to a leak in British Intelligence, the *Sigurimi* knew the identities of all the agents who had participated in the failed *coup d'etat*.

Dushku was unaware that they had learned of his current whereabouts—a local communist agent in Emilia-Romagna had by chance identified Dushku while he was reconnoitering the race route.

When they were informed of Dushku's location, the *Sigurimi* reacted quickly.

They instructed the agent to follow him, and to continue to report on his position.

Once they realized that Dushku was following the progress of the race, they finalized their plan of attack, and they were now closing in on him…

CHAPTER TWENTY-EIGHT

The course through the Veneto—from *Vicenza* to Auronzo-di-Cadore—would be a last reprieve for the riders, before the steep ascents into the snow-covered Dolomite mountains.

From there, they would then contest with the numerous treacherous climbs and descents at the bitterly cold Stelvio Pass.

Ferraro and his confederates had been strangely silent for several days, seemingly content to maintain their position, and to avoid contact with Fausto and his team.

The prudent course of action for this stage would have been to adopt a moderate pace and save themselves for the impending precipitous climbs the next day.

But riding out of Vicenza, the Ferraro team went on the attack, and they moved up through the field with precision and determination.

The remaining French riders had joined their group, and they assisted them with progressing their placement.

When Fausto and his squad saw them approaching, they accepted the challenge, and they set their own pace line, relentlessly hammering away the *kilometres*.

This was old-fashioned raw road racing, and the spectators flanking the route—sensing the rise in tempo—grew delirious with anticipation, and they enthusiastically cheered them on.

However, the overly strenuous exertion took its toll on both teams.

This error in judgment had the result that ten *kilometres* short of the finish they had already burned up all their energy, and with other racers passing them by, they limped across the line.

CHAPTER TWENTY-NINE

In Trentino-Alto-Adige, which is also called the *Sudtyrol* (South Tyrol), the city of Bolzano is known as the gateway to the Dolomites.

To reach the stage finish at the track in Bolzano, the racers would first have to conquer the major elevations and treacherous descents at Misurina, Falzarego, Pordoi and Sella.

Fausto was a relentless climber who excelled in the mountains, and he was motivated to perform well that day as a tribute to his departed mentor Sante, who had loved this region of Italy.

In the remote areas of the race, spectators were often few and far between, and no observers witnessed his heroic pace as Fausto attacked the forbidding ascents.

Nor did any race watchers see Dushku preparing to trigger an avalanche when Fausto approached his position. But the hunter, was himself being hunted…

Julian Gjokana had grown up in the Balkans, and he had learned stealthy hunting skills from an early age.

A former criminal, he was now an elite assassin for the *Sigurimi*.

He had patiently stalked Dushku for several days, and he had decided to take down his prey in these desolate mountains...

As Fausto approached, from an overhanging escarpment Dushku reached to push a boulder he had positioned to cause the landslide.

Just as Dushku began to set off the chain reaction, he felt a strong shove from behind him…

With a loud scream, Dushku and the boulder went over the precipice, bouncing into other rocks which broke loose, and became a roaring mass of rubble that rolled onto, and over the roadway.

Warned by Dushku's yell, Fausto had immediately pulled up to determine what was happening, and he heard the ominous reverberations of the approaching slide just before it swept over the road right in front of him.

He did not see Dushku's body, which was covered by the debris, but he was unnerved, and he was not convinced that the shout he had heard had been only a warning.

But alone on the mountain, there was nothing he could do except proceed…

Fearful of another rockfall, and anxious to get away from the area, with a wary glance at the mountainside he carefully picked his way through the scree, and he resumed his descent…

From the hollow where he had hidden himself, Gjokana had watched with grim satisfaction as Dushku tumbled down the ridge and was crushed by large boulders.

At Sella, Fausto caught up to the lone rider who had been ahead of him, and they jockeyed for the lead as they descended to Bolzano.

When Fausto entered the *velodrome*, invigorated by the cheering *tifosi* he sprinted to the finish, and he triumphantly won the stage.

CHAPTER THIRTY

Riding out of Bolzano, the racers proceeded toward Bormio in *Lombardia* (Lombardy), well-aware, that they were heading to another precipitous climb up along cobblestone paved roads to the Stelvio Pass, known as the *montagna-di-troppo*— "the mountain that is too much."

All the riders were still weary from the strenuous course in the Dolomites the previous day.

The rough-cut uneven road surface took its toll, producing almost constant bone-jarring vibrations, and it was treacherously slick in places.

At this high Alpine elevation in the Ortles mountains, in some places they passed by newly plowed walls of snow that were four *metres* high.

As Fausto and Ferraro ascended, their nearest competitors were over a *kilometre* behind them.

Exhausted, struggling with the tortuous climbs,

and numerous switchbacks, they plodded on.

They tried to ignore the tortuous pain that they felt throughout their bodies from the constant shuddering transmitted from their wheels to their handlebars and bicycle frames.

The two contestants laboriously proceeded- pedal stroke, after pedal stroke- each moment of strained effort isolated in time.

Silently, *mano-a-mano*, they contended the mountain, the only sounds their labored breathing, and the occasional eerie whistle of the frigid wind as it meandered around the peaks...

As they crossed over the summit, Fausto was in the lead, but Ferraro dug deep into his remaining reserves of energy, and he managed to pass him.

Fausto then tried to catch Ferraro, gaining speed as he rode down the dizzying switchbacks.

He fleetingly saw a small stone cross with withered flowers arranged by the roadside—a somber reminder of past tragedy...

The seemingly endless descents became a blur, but Fausto gritted his teeth and endured the punishment.

Throwing caution to the wind, crouched against his bike as if it were a physical manifestation of his will to win, he rode like a man possessed, faster and faster as he flew down the mountainside.

At the end, to Ferraro's astonishment Fausto dared all, and he steered a line inside Ferraro's apex through a dangerous curve.

He resoundingly defeated Ferraro, who afterward looked gaunt and haunted- a beaten man...

Judging from his appearance, Fausto thought that

Ferraro must have misjudged his dosage and taken too many amphetamines.

CHAPTER THIRTY-ONE

The twenty-first, and final Stage of the 1953 *Giro d'Italia*, went from Bormio to *Milano* (Milan), and finished in the *Velodromo Vigorelli*, which had been rebuilt after having been bombed and burned down during the war.

Another Italian rider was the first to cross the finish line and win the final stage, but Fausto had already clinched the overall victory, and he was declared the- *campionissimo* (champion).

Though physically drained by the cumulative effects from his strenuous exertions and excessive drug use, he had endured the intense rigors of the long race and had earned his fifth *Giro* victory.

To this day, among teams and competitors there exists in professional bicycle racing an unspoken code of silence regarding drug usage, and unethical tactics.

At the urging of Campagnolo and his father,

Fausto swore his team to silence about what had transpired during the race with Team Ferraro.

It was sufficient in their estimation that Ferraro and his minions would forever suffer the ignominy of having been vanquished in Italy's greatest bicycle race, both before their countrymen who had attended and witnessed the race, and via television and newspaper coverage, which presented the results around the world...

EPILOGUE

When Fausto returned to his hotel that evening, awaiting him in his room was a basket from the Ferraro bakery, with a loaf of *Piccia Calabrese* (Calabrian bread), an aged *Cacioricotta* goat's milk cheese, and a bottle of *Ciro Rosso Classico* wine.

There was no accompanying note, and he would never know if this gift had been sent to him to acknowledge his win, or if it had been intended for Ferraro, and mis-delivered...

Perhaps the original intent had been for this to go to Ferraro to celebrate his success, and when that result had not come to fruition, it had been rerouted to him instead—to belatedly accept and recognize his victory...

Either way, after suffering the deprivations of the torturous race he thoroughly enjoyed the delicious morsels and rustic wine, before departing to join

Giulia and his team for a well-deserved celebration!

Please enjoy the prologue of
The Concours Caper

PROLOGUE

The Pledge

Shortly after the United States entered the Second World War, two non-commissioned army officers from Chicago were conscripted as agents into the newly formed Counter-Intelligence Corps (CIC).

They were appointed to the American Expeditionary Force in France and acted as insurgents to disrupt the infrastructure for the port city of Bordeaux.

During one of their missions, they took shelter in an abandoned cellar during a bombing attack.

Fortuitously, their shared love of wine began that afternoon.

While huddled together in dim candlelight, they discovered old dust covered bottles which they opened and imbibed as they listened to the explosions above them.

The walls shook violently with each detonation and dust filled the air making it difficult to breathe.

Nonetheless, over the course of several hours they thoroughly enjoyed the impromptu tasting.

As they sipped and savored the wine, both because of its alluring flavor, and with the realization that each swallow might be their last taste of life, they made a pact.

If they survived the night, and the remainder of the conflict, they would learn more about fine wine.

When they returned home after the war, they kept in touch and helped each other build prosperous businesses.

Now they planned to revisit Europe together on a lavish vacation to celebrate their success.

At a black-tie wine tasting dinner at the posh Everglades Club in Palm Beach they hatched a plan.

They agreed a gentlemanly wager for a rare magnum large format bottle of 1945 Chateau Mouton-Rothschild as the prize!

The contest, which would take place over the course of sixty days, would determine which of them could best covertly embarrass an affluent cad that they both abhorred!

The subject of this surreptitious operation was a haughty former French army officer named Guillaume Fouquet.

They had been introduced to Fouquet at military briefings in London during the war when he was attached to General Charles de Gaulle's retinue.

He was the scion of an aristocratic family from the Loire Valley, and an instructor for the elite *Cadre Noir* cavalry corps at the prestigious military equestrian academy - *École Nationale d'Équitation,* located in the town of Saumur.

In their estimation, he was a malefactor who had dishonorably taken advantage of an impressionable young nurse when she was serving in field hospitals near the location where they had been billeted.

She subsequently fell on hard times due to her unrequited love when Fouquet jilted her.

Their intention was for this mission of revenge against Fouquet to be a noble endeavor, and the tactics were to be non-violent and subtle, with a comedic and embarrassing effect.

Their "marching orders" would adhere to- *no harm, no foul*, a term coined that year in the context of the sport of basketball when a referee decided not to call a foul because the contact was not serious enough to affect the outcome of the game.

As with their previous assignments during the war, the ends would justify the means!

Rather than just contribute to another charitable cause, they chose this somewhat novel scheme to privately commemorate the achievement of their financial fortunes, and to relive their experience as spies with this clandestine good deed.

Revenge for the wronged lady, and comeuppance for the effete Frenchman who they despised!

They would have some laughs at their nemesis' expense, and exorcize their long-standing vendetta against him...

ABOUT THE AUTHOR

In his youth, E. Robert Brooks worked in several shops that specialized in the sales and maintenance of high-end racing bicycles. Through these apprenticeships, he gained an appreciation for the craftsmanship that defined that eras custom-made racing machines, and cutting-edge lightweight componentry. He was an amateur racer, and frame builder, and played bicycle polo.

During his travels in Europe and America in the 1970s and 1980s, which included extensive bicycle touring trips, Brooks visited the workshops of several famed artisan frame builders. Subsequently, over the years, as a hobby, he collected and restored antique handmade vintage racing bicycles. At its height, his collection included over sixty rare examples.

E. Robert Brooks' mother was noted journalist - Jane Gregory Brooks.

www.ingramcontent.com/pod-product-compliance
Lightning Source LLC
Chambersburg PA
CBHW071627140626
46555CB00021B/1220